WHERE DOES KITTY GO IN THE RAIN?

Text copyright © 2015 by Harriet Ziefert
Illustrations copyright © 2015 by Brigette Barrager
All rights reserved / CIP date is available.
Published in the United States by
Blue Apple Books
515 Valley Street, Maplewood, NJ 07040
www.blueapplebooks.com

First Edition
Printed in China 03/15
ISBN: 978-1-60905-519-6
1 3 5 7 9 10 8 6 4 2

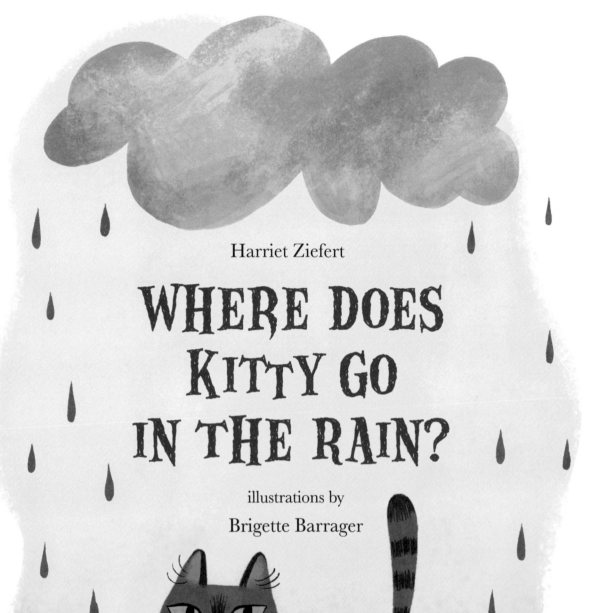

Harriet Ziefert

WHERE DOES KITTY GO IN THE RAIN?

illustrations by

Brigette Barrager

Mommy, Mommy, where's my pet?

Kitty's outside getting wet.

WHAT IS RAIN?

When water heats up,
it turns into warm,
wet air called vapor.

Vapor rises into the
sky, where it becomes
cold and turns into
a cloud.

The cloud becomes
bigger until it is
so heavy that parts
of it fall to the ground.

What falls?
Raindrops!

DO CATS LIKE RAIN?

No! Water makes a cat's fur feel very heavy.

Cats' ears cannot keep water out, and they don't like the way it smells.

For Kitty, it's rain, rain go away!

Kitty will find a place that's dry.

Let's look for Kitty. Want to try?

DO DUCKS LIKE RAIN?

When ducks "comb" their feathers with their bills, they leave a layer of oil on top.

The oil makes water slide off. It keeps the feathers that are closest to the duck's body dry and warm.

In a lake or in the rain, ducks are waterproof!

Raindrops are falling on Mama Duck.

She likes the wet and mushy muck.

DO SQUIRRELS LIKE RAIN?

If it is not raining too hard, a squirrel will curl its tail over its head to make a built-in umbrella!

In heavy rains, squirrels stay in their nests to keep dry.

Rain won't scare a squirrel away.

He stays busy on a rainy day.

Brown beetle's shell is shiny and hard.

DO BEETLES
LIKE RAIN?

A beetle has
a hard, shell-like
covering that
prevents it from
getting soaked.

He doesn't mind a rainy yard.

DO WORMS LIKE RAIN?

Yes!
Earthworms
mostly live and
travel underground,
because they need
moisture—
all the time.

After it rains,
you will see
worms because
it is wet enough
for them. They can
wriggle along
much faster
above ground.

Worms are squirmy
on wet ground.

They squirm and wiggle all around.

Under leaves two butt...st

DO BUTTERFLIES LIKE RAIN?

Rain makes butterflies too cold to fly. They hide out in protected spots, called roosts, until the storm passes.

When the sun comes out, so do the butterflies!

Keeping wings dry is what's best.

Bird peeks out from a hole in a tree.

He says, "Look! No rain on me!"

DO BIRDS LIKE RAIN?

Some do;
some don't.

Most small birds
tuck themselves
away in nests,
or the inner
branches of a tree
or bush, or under
anything that will
keep the rain off.

After a rainstorm
passes, you can
go outside and
listen for all
the birdie-chirps!

Mommy, Mommy, look at that.

I think I spy my kitty cat!

WHERE DID KITTY GO?

Look through the book. Can you find a thick bush, a birdbath, a pail, a red doghouse, and a brown shed?

Which is the best rainy-day hiding place for Kitty?

Clouds are gone.
The sun is high.

Here's my kitty, warm and dry!

WHAT DO YOU DO
WHEN IT RAINS?

Stay inside?

Put on a raincoat
and boots?

Use an umbrella?

Catch raindrops
on your tongue?

Stomp in a puddle?

Which of these
do you like to do?

RAINY-DAY WONDERS

Compare & Contrast

A duck likes the rain; a squirrel does not.
Find out what about each animal makes this so.

Take out your rain clothes. Compare your rain clothes to the feathers,
shells and skin of animals that don't mind being in the rain.
How do your clothes help you stay dry?

Research

How much rain falls on a rainy day? When you think it is going to rain,
place a paper cup outside where the rain can fall freely
(without trees or rooftops in the way) into the cup. After the rain, check
how much rain has fallen. Mark the line of rain and the date on the cup.
Repeat with the same cup on the next rainy day.

Find out why clouds produce raindrops.
What makes thunder? What makes lightning?

Observe

Go back and find out how the animals in this book sheltered from the rain. Imagine it raining inside your house. What could you do to make shelter? Can you make a shelter with a blanket?

Have a raindrop race. Choose two raindrops and see which runs to the bottom of the window first.

Write, Tell, or Draw

Write about or draw the same spot outdoors before the rain, during the rain, and after the rain.

Make a list of rainy-day words. Ask others for words they think of for rain and rainy days.

Draw or tell a story about the animals in this book gathering for a tea party to drink rainwater tea. Use your own stuffed animals to make a "Rainwater Tea Party."